SECRET AGENT

JACK STALWART

The Mission to Find Max:
EGYPT

Join Secret Agent Jack Stalwart

on his other adventures:

The Search for the Sunken Treasure: **AUSTRALIA**

The Secret of the Sacred Temple: **CAMBODIA**

The Escape of the Deadly Dinosaur: **USA**

The Puzzle of the Missing Panda: **CHINA**

The Mystery of the Mona Lisa: **FRANCE**

The Caper of the Crown Jewels: **ENGLAND**

Peril at the Grand Prix: **ITALY**

The Pursuit of the Ivory Poachers: **KENYA**

The Deadly Race to Space: **RUSSIA**

The Quest for Aztec Gold: **MEXICO**

The Theft of the Samurai Sword: **JAPAN**

The Fight for the Frozen Land: **ARCTIC**

The Hunt for the Yeti Skull: **NEPAL**

The Mission to Find Max: EGYPT

Elizabeth Singer Hunt

Illustrated by Brian Williamson

WEINSTEIN
BOOKS

ISBN: 978-1-60286-152-7
E-Book ISBN: 978-1-60286-156-5

First Edition

10 9 8 7 6 5 4 3

To the children who have patiently waited
for this conclusion, this is for you

THE WORLD

Destination:
EGYPT

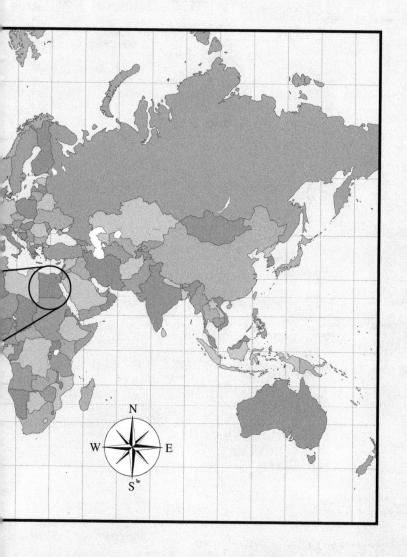

JACK STALWART

Jack Stalwart applied to be a secret agent for the Global Protection Force four months ago.

My name is Jack Stalwart. My older brother, Max, was a secret agent for you, until he disappeared on one of your missions. Now I want to be a secret agent too. If you choose me, I will be an excellent secret agent and get rid of evil villains, just like my brother did.

Sincerely,

Jack Stalwart

GLOBAL PROTECTION FORCE INTERNAL MEMO:
HIGHLY CONFIDENTIAL

Jack Stalwart was sworn in as a Global Protection Force secret agent four months ago. Since that time, he has completed all of his missions successfully and has stopped no less than twelve evil villains. Because of this he has been assigned the code name 'COURAGE'.

Jack has yet to uncover the whereabouts of his brother, Max, who is still working for this organization at a secret location. Do not give Secret Agent Jack Stalwart this information. He is never to know about his brother.

Gerald Barter

Gerald Barter
Director, Global Protection Force

THINGS YOU'LL FIND IN EVERY BOOK

Watch Phone: The only gadget Jack wears all the time, even when he's not on official business. His Watch Phone is the central gadget that makes most others work. There are lots of important features, most importantly the 'C' button, which reveals the code of the day – necessary to unlock Jack's Secret Agent Book Bag. There are buttons on both sides, one of which ejects his life-saving Melting Ink Pen. Beyond these functions, it also works as a phone and, of course, gives Jack the time of day.

Global Protection Force (GPF): The GPF is the organization Jack works for. It's a worldwide force of young secret agents whose aim is to protect the world's people, places and possessions. No one knows exactly where its main offices are located (all correspondence and gadgets for repair are sent to a special PO Box, and training is held at various locations around the world), but Jack thinks it's somewhere cold, like the Arctic Circle.

Whizzy: Jack's magical miniature globe. Almost every night at precisely 7:30 p.m., the GPF uses Whizzy to send Jack the identity of the country that he must travel to. Whizzy can't talk, but he can cough up messages. Jack's parents don't know Whizzy is anything more than a normal globe.

The Magic Map: The magical map hanging on Jack's bedroom wall. Unlike most maps, the GPF's map is made of a mysterious wood. Once Jack inserts the country piece from Whizzy, the map swallows Jack whole and sends him away on his missions. When he returns, he arrives precisely one minute after he left.

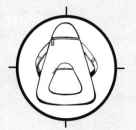

Secret Agent Book Bag: The Book Bag that Jack wears on every adventure. Licensed only to GPF secret agents, it contains top-secret gadgets necessary to foil bad guys and escape certain death. To activate the bag before each mission, Jack must punch in a secret code given to him by his Watch Phone. Once he's away, all he has to do is place his finger on the zip, which identifies him as the owner of the bag and immediately opens.

THE STALWART FAMILY

Jack's dad, John

He moved the family to England when Jack was two, in order to take a job with an aerospace company. Jack's dad thinks he is an ordinary boy and that his other son, Max, attends a school in Switzerland. Jack's dad is American and his mom is British, which makes Jack a bit of both.

Jack's mom, Corinne

One of the greatest moms as far as Jack is concerned. When she and her husband received a letter from a posh school in Switzerland inviting Max to attend, they were overjoyed. Since Max left six months ago, they have received numerous notes in Max's handwriting telling them he's OK. Little do they know it's all a lie and that it's the GPF sending those letters.

Jack's older brother, Max

Two years ago, at the age of nine, Max joined the GPF. Max used to tell Jack about his adventures and show him how to work his secret-agent gadgets. When the family received a letter inviting Max to attend a school in Europe, Jack figured it was to do with the GPF. Max told him he was right, but that he couldn't tell Jack anything about why he was going away.

Nine-year-old Jack Stalwart

Four months ago, Jack received an anonymous note saying: 'Your brother is in danger. Only you can save him.' As soon as he could, Jack applied to be a secret agent too. Since that time, he's battled some of the world's most dangerous villains, and hopes some day in his travels to find and rescue his brother, Max.

DESTINATION:
Egypt

Egypt is one of the oldest civilizations in the world. It started around 3150 BC when the pharaoh Menes united lower and upper Egypt.

●

Cairo is Egypt's capital city. It is located next to the Nile, the longest river in the world.

●

People in Egypt speak Arabic, although some also speak English and French.

The pyramids at Giza, the Sphinx and the tombs in the Valley of the Kings are some of Egypt's most famous monuments.

●

Ancient Egyptians wrote on a paper-like material called 'papyrus', which was made from the papyrus plant.

The Great Travel Guide

SECRET AGENT PHRASE BOOK
FOR EGYPT

What is your name?
Masmuk?
(pronounced mas-MUK)

My name is...
Ismi
(pronounced IS-mi)

Hello
Marhaban
(pronounced
mar-HA-ban)

Thank you
Shukran
(pronounced
SHU-kran)

Goodbye
Ma-a salama
(pronounced
Ma-A Sala-ma)

GPF FACTS: KING TUT

King Tut's original name was Tutankhaten,
but he later changed his name to
Tutankhamun. He was born in 1341 BC.

Tutankhamun's family was the
eighteenth family to rule Egypt.

King Tut became pharaoh at eight
or nine years old. He died at the
age of nineteen.

GPF FACTS: KING TUT

King Tut's father, Akhenaten, tried to change Egyptian religion so that people worshipped one god only – Aten, the disk of the sun. When King Tut became pharaoh, he allowed people to worship many gods again, which made him popular with his people.

Nobody knows what caused King Tut's death, but scientists think he died from an infection caused by a broken leg.

King Tut is one of the most famous 'mummies' in the world. In 1922, an archaeologist named Howard Carter discovered his tomb almost completely intact.

GPF Facts: The Valley of the Kings

The Valley of the Kings was the burial place for the kings and nobles of Egypt from the sixteenth to the eleventh century BC.

The Valley is on the west bank of the Nile, across from the ancient city of Thebes (now called Luxor).

There are more than sixty tombs and hundreds of chambers. Only twenty kings were actually buried there; the rest are nobles.

The first pharaoh to be buried there was Thutmose I. The last pharaoh to be buried there was Ramses XI.

GPF Guide: How Mummies were made

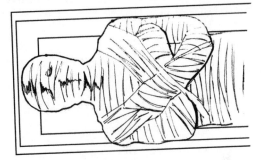

In ancient Egypt, the body of an important person was preserved so that his or her soul could recognize it later.

The person who preserved the body was called an 'embalmer'.

The embalmer washed the body in the Nile River and took out the person's organs. Organs were placed in 'canopic jars'. Natron salt was used to dry out the body.

Resin-soaked linens were put inside. Make-up and a wig were added, and oils like myrrh were used to perfume it. A pine resin was brushed on top.

Finally, the embalmer wrapped the body in linen. Amulets, a mask, an identifying tab and a copy of the Book of the Dead were all buried with the mummy.

SECRET AGENT GADGET INSTRUCTION MANUAL

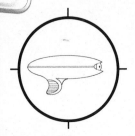

Laser Burst: The GPF's Laser Burst is a handheld laser that emits a powerful white light capable of slicing through almost anything. Perfect when you need to burn a quick hole, start a campfire or cut through something hard.

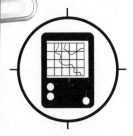

Map Mate: When you're lost or need to get somewhere fast, use the GPF's Map Mate. This clever gadget receives signals from satellites in space to give you a map of any country or city in the world. It can also show you how to get from one place to another using directional arrows to guide the way.

Long-tail Boat:

The GPF's Long-tail Boat is perfect when you need to travel across long distances on water. Modelled after riverboats in Southeast Asia that use a long pole at the back for steering, the GPF's Long-tail Boat can travel at speeds of 50mph. After dropping the toy version into the water, it transforms to the real, full-sized thing. As soon as you step out, it changes back to a toy.

Time Release Vapors:

Whenever another secret agent or trusted contact has been knocked out, use the Time Release Vapors to restore them to consciousness. Just open the tub, place a small amount of cream on your finger and rub it under the agent's nose. The vapors should work within seconds.

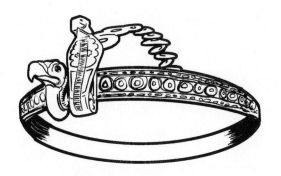

Chapter 1:
The Treasure Hunt

It was a Friday afternoon and Jack
Stalwart was standing with his Fourth
Grade class in the lobby of the British
Museum in London. Not only did the
British Museum hold more than one
million artifacts from the ancient world,
it didn't cost a thing to visit. Jack and his
classmates were on a field trip studying
its treasures.

'OK, everyone,' said Jack's history
teacher, Mr Marshall. He was handing out

pieces of paper to each pupil. 'The curator of the museum has arranged a treasure hunt for us.'

The students cheered and clapped.

'We're going to split you into six teams,' he said. 'The first team to find all thirteen objects wins a prize.'

Mr Marshall organized his class into groups of three. Luckily for Jack, he was paired up with two of the cleverest pupils in the class, his best friends Richard and Charlie.

'Let's crush 'em,' said Richard.

'Yeah,' said Charlie. 'They don't stand a chance.'

Mr Marshall looked at his watch. 'Time starts'– he said as he waited for the second hand to pass the twelve– 'now!'

Jack, Richard and Charlie quickly looked at the first clue on the paper:

A VALUABLE KEY IN DECIPHERING EGYPTIAN HIEROGLYPHIC WRITING CAN BE FOUND IN ROOM 4. WHAT IS IT CALLED?

'I know,' whispered Charlie, so the other teams couldn't hear. 'It's the Rosetta Stone.'

Not having to find Room 4 saved them some time. Jack scribbled the answer in the space next to question one. The second clue, however, was much harder.

WHICH ISLAND IS FAMOUS FOR ITS STONE STATUES CALLED 'MOAI'? YOU CAN FIND THE ANSWER IN ROOM 24.

Jack, Richard and Charlie looked at each other blankly. According to the map, Room 24 was down the corridor ahead, next to the bookshop. They raced for it, and when they got there, they saw an enormous stone statue with the face of a man. Underneath it was a sign that said:

> HOA HAKANANAI'A
> STATUE FROM EASTER ISLAND

Richard noted the name 'Easter' in the blank next to question two. Charlie read question three out loud:

IN 31 BC THIS EMPEROR CAPTURED EGYPT FOR THE ROMANS. WHO WAS HE? VISIT ROOM 70 TO FIND OUT.

Unfortunately Jack didn't know much about Greek or Roman history. The junior crime-fighting agency that Jack worked for, the GPF, had taught him many things, but most of it was practical stuff, like how to stop a bad guy from coming at you with a poison pen. He shrugged his shoulders at his friends and took the lead, climbing the stairs to the upper floor.

When the boys got to Room 70, they found themselves in the Roman Empire section. Perched on a pedestal in the middle of the room was the marble head of a man with glass eyes.

The sign underneath said:

AUGUSTUS, WHO DEFEATED
MARK ANTONY AND CLEOPATRA
TO CLAIM EGYPT FOR THE ROMANS

'That's it!' said Richard, scribbling down the name 'Augustus'.

The boys carried on scouring the museum and finding the answers to the next nine questions. It took nearly forty-five minutes, but finally they were staring at question thirteen.

DURING MUMMIFICATION, ANCIENT EGYPTIAN EMBALMERS PLACED THE ORGANS OF THE DECEASED IN 'CANOPIC' JARS. WHICH BABOON-HEADED GOD'S JAR CONTAINED THE LIVER? YOU CAN FIND THE ANSWER IN ROOM 62.

The trio were in a hurry now. There were at least four other groups nearby who were close to finishing the treasure hunt as well.

Jack, Richard and Charlie dashed up the steps to the third floor. Out of breath, they frantically looked for the answer to the question. But there was nothing obvious.

'Let's split up,' said Charlie. 'I'll look over here,' he said, pointing to a collection of tall glass cases. 'You guys take the other side of the room.'

The boys separated. Soon Jack found himself gazing at treasures from the tombs of ancient Egyptian kings. One of them was a gilded chair from the tomb of the pharaoh Tutankhamun, or King Tut. At the sight of that name, the hairs on Jack's arms stood straight up.

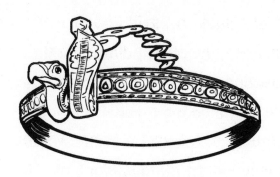

Chapter 2:
The Diadem

A few months ago, Jack had received a note saying that his brother, Max, was in danger and that only Jack could save him from whatever peril he was in.

As soon as Jack had received the note, he had joined the secret agent organization his brother was working for, the Global Protection Force (or GPF), and set about trying to find clues to his brother's disappearance.

The GPF refused to tell Jack a thing, but

on two previous missions, he had collected clues that pointed to Max being somewhere in Egypt. His brother had also sent him a coded typewritten note that Jack had deciphered into the words 'Thebes' and 'Tutankhamon'.

Jack knew that Thebes was the ancient name for the city of Luxor in Egypt and that Tutankhamun was the name of the famous boy king who had ruled Egypt from 1333 to 1324 BC.

But what he didn't understand was why his brother spelled King Tut's name with an 'o' instead of the usual 'u'. Or why he had used an old-fashioned typewriter instead of a computer. Plus, what was Max doing in Egypt in the first place?

Whatever the reason, Jack figured that Max's mission was important. After all, the GPF had faked a school in Switzerland for Max to go to. In the history of the GPF they'd only sent three agents, including Max, away from their families for an extended period of time.

Mary Biden had been sent to the Amazon rainforest to live with the natives and spy on some nasty oil companies that were making the water toxic  and the villagers sick. The information she returned with two months later led to a lawsuit that had closed the companies down.

Jeremy Bradford was sent to the Bermuda Triangle to

discover the whereabouts of some missing ships. He was probably still there because nobody had heard from him since.

For everyone else, being away for a long time wasn't necessary. The GPF could send you on a mission and return you to your home one minute after you'd left. Time travelling was a way to keep kids happy and their parents in the dark.

As soon as Max had left for 'school', the GPF started sending notes from 'Max' to Jack's parents. The letters were supposed to be in Max's handwriting, but Jack knew they had been forged by Louise Persnall, the secretary to the Director of the GPF. That's because Jack had used the Signature ID to identify her. The Signature ID was a GPF gadget that used a worldwide database of handwriting samples. He'd also used the Signature ID to confirm that Max had indeed sent that coded note.

Looking at King Tut's chair in the glass case, Jack started to wonder whether Max's mission had something to do with the treasures of King Tut. Maybe Max was protecting King Tut himself. Now that would be a mission, thought Jack.

Unfortunately, the only way Jack was going to answer that question was to actually go to Egypt. But he couldn't very well jump on a plane. He didn't have enough money to buy a ticket, and he couldn't leave home without scaring his parents silly. He was going to have to wait until a stroke of luck opened a door of possibility.

Just then, a voice interrupted Jack's thoughts.

'Find anything?' yelled Richard.

'No,' said Jack. 'Not yet.'

'Me neither,' said Charlie from the other side of the room.

Jack turned back to the glass case with the chair. Next to it was another case containing four small jars. He walked over to it and noticed that there was a sign beside them:

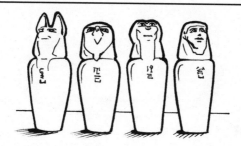

'I've got something!' Jack shouted to his friends.

Richard and Charlie rushed over. 'Brilliant!' said Charlie, clapping Jack on the back. He quickly wrote the answer 'Hapi' on the page. 'You did it. Let's get going.'

Richard and Charlie started running as another group rushed out of the room too. Jack was about to join them when something to his right caught his attention. It was a photo on the wall of a crown with a vulture and cobra at the top.

Underneath, there was a story about it:

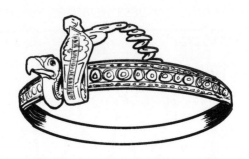

The Mystery of King Tut's Diadem

King Tut was a powerful and influential Egyptian pharaoh. Lots of people worshipped him like a god. On many occasions the young pharaoh wore jewellery and amulets to protect him and convey his power. None was more important than his diadem, or crown. In fact, it was so important that he was buried with it on his head.

When the archaeologist Howard Carter discovered King Tut's tomb in 1922, he

*removed the diadem. But within days it
had disappeared. It was thought to have
been stolen by an assistant of Mr Carter's,
Mr Omar Massri. This, however, has never
been proven.*

*Earlier this year, the diadem was found
again, and placed in the care of the
archaeologist Rachel Newington. Shortly
after, it vanished again. The location and
true power of King Tut's diadem is one of
the greatest mysteries of ancient Egypt.*

Jack finished reading the sign and
gasped. Rachel Newington was the name
of the lady he'd met on a mission in
Cambodia. Mrs Newington had been
kidnapped by a man with gold teeth who
was seeking the power of an ancient
Khmer necklace. Jack had worked with her
daughter, Kate, to locate Rachel and stop
the man from taking the necklace away.

17

After Jack saved Rachel's life, she'd given him a clue about his brother: Max had been helping her protect something in Egypt, but one day both the object and Max disappeared. Soon afterwards, Rachel had been sent to Cambodia.

After reading this, Jack was pretty sure that his brother had been involved in protecting the diadem. After all, the facts of the story seemed to fit. Plus, it was the kind of job that a GPF agent would be asked to do.

'Jack,' said a voice from behind him. It was one of the parent helpers. 'Mr Marshall wants everyone downstairs.'

'OK.' Jack hurried down the stairs and back to the lobby. When he got there, he saw one of the teams waving a fancy book in the air. Richard and Charlie stood beside them with sour looks on their faces.

'I guess we didn't win,' said Jack, walking over to his friends.

'It's all because of you,' sulked Richard. 'Mr Marshall said that we had to return as a team. If you'd been here, we would have won.'

'Sorry,' said Jack. 'I got distracted.'

Charlie and Richard stomped off. Richard looked over his shoulder at Jack

and shouted, 'Hope it was worth it!'

'It was,' Jack whispered to himself.

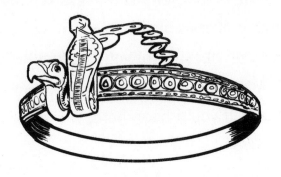

Chapter 3:
The King's Falcon

Richard, Charlie and the rest of the class
headed for the outdoor courtyard. Mr
Marshall was busy organizing the kids
and the parent helpers.

'Everybody gather together!' he said.
'The bus leaves in two minutes.'

As Jack made his way over, he noticed
a crowd of people to his right. They were
standing in front of a large oak tree,
pointing up at one of the branches. Jack
craned his neck up, and saw a beautiful

bird of prey perched on one of the limbs.
Since there was a bit of time to kill, Jack
went over. He could hear the people
chatting.

'In all my years as a bird watcher,' said an elderly man, 'I've never seen a bird like this before.'

'It's so regal,' said a woman. 'What do you reckon it is?'

'Some sort of falcon,' replied the man.

It was certainly unusual. It had a dark blue head, green wings and a white breast. As Jack stared at the bird, it turned its head and gazed at him with piercing eyes.

The old man nudged him. 'He seems to have taken a liking to you,' he said.

'Yeah,' said Jack, feeling uncomfortable. They weren't called birds of prey for nothing.

Keeping its eyes fixed on Jack, the bird spread its wings and flapped up off the branch. It soared high into the sky, then circled majestically over the courtyard. The crowd gasped in awe.

Then, suddenly, the falcon changed direction and dived towards the crowd, its talons outstretched. It was going in for a kill!

'Get down!' yelled Jack. 'Cover your necks!'

Everyone fell to the ground in panic, and covered their head with their hands. The next thing Jack knew, something sharp scraped against his fingers. He looked out of the corner of his eye and saw the falcon soaring up into the air, circling around for another attempt.

Spying a plant pot nearby, Jack grabbed a handful of stones that were sitting on top of the soil. He stood up as the falcon dived again and started throwing stones at it. Most of them missed, but one hit the bird square in the chest, making it screech in anger, pull away and fly off southwards.

Jack and the others waited for it to return, but it disappeared into the distance. Everyone relaxed, and stood up again. 'He nearly took your head off!' said the twitcher to Jack. 'At the very least you'll need to get that taken care of.' The man nodded down to Jack's fingers, which were scratched and bleeding. Jack had been so focused on getting rid of the bird that he hadn't realized he'd been hurt.

'Dude,' said Richard, walking over. 'That bird almost snatched you. I saw it with my own eyes.'

One of the parent helpers rushed over to Jack with a first aid kit. She quickly began to wrap his fingers in sterile gauze. 'You'll need to see the nurse when you get back to school,' she said.

'Hurry, children!' yelled Mr Marshall, hustling his pupils towards the bus. 'Let's get on before there's any more trouble.'

Still in shock, Jack clambered onto the bus and settled into his seat. Richard and Charlie were talking about what they'd seen in the courtyard.

'Did you see its beak?!' said Charlie. 'It was huge!'

'It was this close to flying off with Jack!' said Richard, putting two fingers an inch apart.

Jack wasn't sure about that, but he was sure of one thing. That bird was definitely targeting *him*. But why?

He told himself the answer didn't matter. After all, he was safely on the bus now. There was no way he was going to see that bird again. At least, he hoped not.

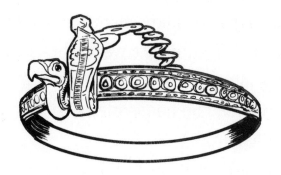

Chapter 4:
The Penny Portal

Compared to being attacked by a bird, the rest of the day was pretty uneventful. Jack came home at 3:30 p.m., played a few computer games, ate dinner, and by 7:20 p.m. was heading upstairs. When he got to his room, he wrapped pieces of the GPF's Fix-It tape around his cuts and watched as the clock ticked by to 7:30 p.m. His miniature globe, Whizzy, was still asleep, snoozing on Jack's bedside table.

Whenever the GPF had a mission for

Jack, Whizzy would wake up at 7:30 p.m., and cough a country-shaped jigsaw piece out of his mouth. Jack would then slot the piece into the Magic Map of the world on his wall and be transported to his destination.

Since Whizzy was still asleep at 7:32 p.m., Jack was sure he didn't have a mission tonight. He went over to

his desk and opened a drawer. Sliding his hand inside, he tapped the underside and a secret hiding place was revealed. He pulled out some important papers.

Carrying them over to his bed, Jack laid them out on the duvet. The first was the original note he'd received many months ago, telling him that Max was in danger.

The second was an example of a forged note from Max in Louise Persnall's handwriting. The last was the coded note from Max himself.

As he was looking at the letters, something struck Jack. The Signature ID was created after notes from Max started coming home. This meant that Jack had never checked the identity of the person who wrote the first note! Jack shook his head in frustration. He couldn't believe how silly he'd been.

Quickly he tapped his Watch Phone and asked for the code of the day. As soon as the code word FOOTBALL appeared, Jack punched it into the lock on his Book Bag, and opened it.

Pulling out the Signature ID, he scanned it over the letter. It took only seconds, but the name 'Penny Powell' popped up. Jack didn't know anyone named Penny, so he asked the Signature ID to give him more information. When he found out who Penny worked for, he was shocked.

PENNY POWELL

GPF HQ

Penny worked for none other than the GPF. The same organization that he and his brother belonged to! Maybe Penny knew details about Max. Better still, she might help Jack get to Egypt.

Using his Watch Phone, Jack found Penny's phone number in the GPF Employee Directory, and dialled it. A crackling noise came from his Watch Phone. An image of a woman sizzled onto the screen. She was young, probably in her twenties, and more than a little nervous.

'Secret Agent Courage here,' said Jack. 'Are you Penny?'

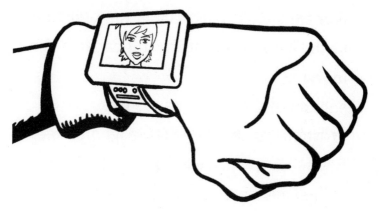

'I've been waiting for you to contact me,' she said, looking quickly over her shoulder. 'I don't have long.'

'What do you know about Max?' asked Jack.

'I used to work for Director Barter,' she said, 'before Louise. I came across your brother's file, and saw that he was in trouble.'

'What kind of trouble?' said Jack.

'Someone was trying to hunt him down,' said Penny. She looked over her shoulder again, then back at the screen. She leaned in closer. 'I told the Director that we should pull Max off the case,' she said. 'That it was getting too dangerous for him.'

'What did he say?' asked Jack.

'Nothing,' said Penny. 'He ignored me. Before I knew it, I was assigned to work with someone else.'

Jack's heart was really thumping now. If what Penny said was true, then Max was all alone. Jack really was his brother's only hope.

'Can you get me to Egypt?' he asked.

There was a noise behind Penny. 'Someone's coming,' she said, looking worried. 'I'll see what I can do.'

Before Jack could say anything else, the image disappeared from the screen.

Just then,
Whizzy woke up,
winked at Jack
and started to
spin. Whizzy
coughed up a
jigsaw piece
and Jack scooped it up. As soon as he
saw its shape, Jack knew that Penny had
managed to help him.

Fitting the shape into the map, Jack
waited for the name 'Egypt' to appear. He
grabbed his Book Bag from underneath
his bed and ran back to the map. The
light inside Egypt was growing brighter
now.

Jack closed his eyes and said a silent
prayer for good luck. When the time was
right, he yelled, 'Off to Egypt!' Then the
light burst, and swallowed him into the
Magic Map.

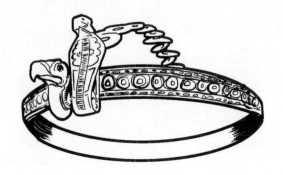

Chapter 5:
The Curator Speaks

The next thing Jack knew, he was standing in the middle of a dusty, busy market place called a souk. Shops were selling just about anything you could imagine — ceramics, coffee, copper pots, dresses and King Tut T-shirts. A donkey cart clip-clopped in front of a queue of taxis.

Usually, when Jack arrived at a location, he had a contact to meet; someone in charge of the operation on the ground.

But this time he was all alone.

Up ahead was a sign:

KHAN AL KHALILI
CAIRO'S 700-YEAR-OLD
MARKETPLACE

Now Jack knew where he was. He was in Cairo, Egypt's capital city. Jack also knew that Cairo was home to one of the most famous museums on King Tut, the Egyptian Museum. Since Max was probably guarding one of King Tut's treasures, Jack thought it would be a good place to start. After all, he needed to find out more about that diadem.

He pulled out the GPF's Map Mate. The Map Mate was a hand-held GPS navigation device that could tell you how to get from point A to point B. He waited

for the device to pick up his signal, then
he told it he needed to get to the
Egyptian Museum.

Within seconds, the Map Mate had
calculated his route. The museum was
only ten minutes away. Jack followed the
arrows, heading southwest through the
noisy streets. Above him, clothes were
strung across on ropes. Vendors were
selling fruits and spices. Men were
blowing horns in an attempt to get cobras
to dance out of their woven baskets.

Finally Jack came to the Nile, one of the

37

most famous rivers in the world. There,
near its banks, was an enormous pink
building — the Egyptian Museum.

Jack passed a copy of the ancient
Sphinx at the front and walked into the
great hall. He plucked a map from the
tourist information center, and found what
he was looking for — the curator's office.

The curator was the boss of the museum, and if anyone had information about the diadem, it would be him.

Jack wandered along the narrow corridors until he came to a door at the back. Hanging on it was a plaque: ALI HASSAN, CURATOR. Jack knocked. A man answered in English. 'Enter,' he said.

Jack opened the door. Sitting at a wooden desk in front of a typewriter was a dark-skinned man wearing glasses and a bushy moustache.

'My name is Jack, and I would like some information for my school project. Do you mind if I ask you a few questions?' asked Jack.

'No, of course not – go ahead,' said Mr Hassan.

'Well,' said Jack, 'I was wondering about King Tut's diadem.'

The curator's eyebrows rose. 'The diadem, huh?' he said. 'It is written that whoever wears the diadem will rule the world.'

Jack's eyebrows rose in return. He had no idea that the diadem possessed so much power. Mr Hassan narrowed his eyes at Jack.

'What school do you go to?' he asked.

For a moment Jack was thrown off guard.

'The reason I ask,' Mr Hassan went on, 'is that another English boy came to see

40

me a few months ago. He too asked
about the diadem. Perhaps you go to the
same school?'

Jack's tummy did a flip-flop. 'What did
he look like?' he asked.

'He was slightly older than you,' said
Mr Hassan, 'with fair hair.'

Jack couldn't believe it. He rifled
through his
trouser
pocket and
pulled out
his wallet.
Inside was a

picture of Jack and Max at the beach. He
showed it to the man.

'Was this him?' he asked.

The curator nodded. 'It seems as
though you're already friends,' he said.

'More than that,' said Jack excitedly
under his breath. 'What did he want?'

'He wanted to know about the history of the diadem,' said Mr Hassan. 'Specifically about who stole it from Howard Carter. I told him what I knew. Howard Carter had an assistant named Omar,' he explained. 'Everyone called him "O". The day after Howard Carter discovered it, Omar and the diadem disappeared.'

Before Jack could say anything, Mr Hassan carried on.

'The diadem was found decades later by a villager in the ancient city of Thebes. The archaeologist Rachel Newington was brought in to care for it. Soon, however, it vanished again.'

Things were starting to fall into place. Max had written the name 'Thebes' in his coded note to Jack. It was likely that he had been in Thebes guarding the diadem with Rachel. This was also where it had been found again.

The letter 'o' was used instead of a 'u' in the common spelling of Tutankhamun. Jack wondered whether Max had put it there as a clue about Omar.

'What else did my, um, friend say?' said Jack.

'He asked whether Omar had any children,' said the curator.

'Anything else?' asked Jack.

'Only that he was feeling ill,' said Mr Hassan. 'The boy asked for a glass of water. So I left him in my office while I went to fetch it. When I came back, he was gone.'

Jack was worried. Maybe Max had some kind of horrible illness. Maybe he needed medical attention. But then Jack noticed the typewriter in front of Mr Hassan.

It was a common secret agent trick to ask for a glass of water so that you were left alone. Maybe it was here that Max had typed that coded letter to Jack. On Mr Hassan's very own typewriter.

Jack smiled, and thanked the curator for the information. Mr Hassan bade Jack farewell and went back to his work.

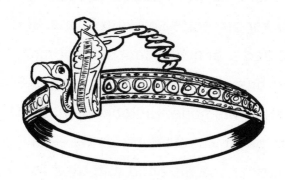

Chapter 6:
The Guardian

When Jack got outside, he saw something incredible. Perched on the back of the Sphinx was a falcon, just like the one he'd seen in England. It was staring at him. Jack started to feel uneasy. If it was the same one, then it was definitely following him.

Suddenly Jack heard laughter. He quickly turned to see who it was, and spotted a bunch of tourists standing next to a bus. When Jack turned back to the bird, it was gone. He looked up at the sky, but it was nowhere to be seen.

Jack shook his head and tried to focus on Max. His brother had come to Cairo to gather information about Omar. But why was Max interested in Omar? Nearly eighty years had passed since Howard Carter discovered King Tut's treasures. And Omar, or 'O', was probably dead by now.

Either way, it was likely that Max had returned to Thebes, which was the ancient name for the city of Luxor. So Jack programmed his Map Mate to calculate the distance between Cairo and Luxor. Unfortunately it was eight hours away.

As he stared at the River Nile in front of

him, Jack had an idea. Reaching into his Book Bag, he pulled out a long toy boat. He dropped it into the Nile, and within moments it had grown to the size of a real boat.

This was the GPF's Longtail Boat. The Longtail could travel at up to fifty miles an hour. And since Jack had to cover a long distance, it was the best gadget for the job.

Jack climbed on board and sat down at the back. With a quick flick of a switch, he was on his way.

Chapter 7:
The Treasure Factory

When Jack arrived in Luxor, he moored the boat to the dock and climbed out. The Longtail Boat immediately shrank back to the size of a toy. He plucked it out of the Nile, and put it back in his Book Bag.

'Where to now?' Jack asked himself.

Up ahead was a sign:

THIS WAY TO THE VALLEY OF THE KINGS

COME AND SEE ARCHAEOLOGICAL
WONDERS UP CLOSE

SALAMA MASSRI, CHIEF ARCHAEOLOGIST

Jack decided to explore. After all, maybe this Massri guy had information about the diadem. Maybe he'd even seen Max.

Jack walked along the dusty path towards the Valley of the Kings. He knew that this was an enormous valley where pharaohs and noble people were buried, from the sixteenth to the eleventh century.

Because robbers had found it easy to steal from the pyramids, the Egyptian kings of the eighteenth to the twentieth dynasties decided to hide their bodies in the valley. That way, it would be more difficult to find them and their treasures.

Little did the kings know that, hundreds of years later, millions of tourists would visit their burial grounds. So would archaeologists. In 1922 Howard Carter

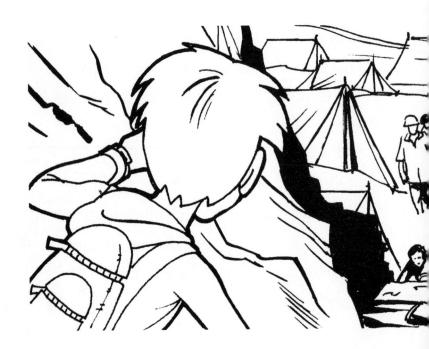

found King Tut's tomb here. From the looks of it, Salama Massri was hoping to become famous too.

Up ahead Jack saw a camp full of tents. Men, women, boys and girls were scurrying everywhere, carrying maps, tools and small objects. Some were sitting at tables, cataloging finds. Others were sifting through sand. It was like a factory; a factory for artifact-hunting.

'Nice work, everyone!' a man was shouting from another tent. 'Remember, whatever we find, we get to keep – I mean, turn over to the museum.'

Jack reckoned that must be Salama Massri. But he couldn't see him yet.

'We need to find ten more artifacts today,' the man was bellowing. 'And you know I don't like to be disappointed.'

The hired hands scurried around even faster. One of the boys bumped into another, causing him to drop what he was working on.

'Careful!' the man roared.

The frightened boy picked up his tools and ran off.

'Everything in this valley is valuable, even the smallest bit of grit,' the man said, stepping out of the tent and smiling at his workers.

As he did so, the sunlight bounced off

his teeth, sending out a blinding ray of light. Jack quickly shielded his eyes with his hand. When the man closed his mouth, the light disappeared. It was then that Jack realized who it was. He nearly fainted on the spot.

Standing in the middle of the camp was none other than the man with the gold teeth; the madman from Cambodia who'd kidnapped Rachel Newington. Jack dropped to his knees and hid behind a table.

'Remember,' the man sneered, 'each of you is responsible for finding something. And if you don't,' he said, kicking sand into a girl's eyes, 'you'll have to answer to me.'

Jack saw an Asian man in silk pantaloons walking over to join Massri. He was the same man who had helped Massri in Cambodia. The two of them left the camp.

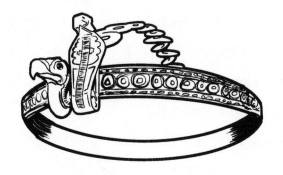

Chapter 8:
The Villain Revealed

Jack's head was spinning. What was the man with the gold teeth doing in Egypt? The last time Jack had seen him, he was being hauled away by the Cambodian police. Maybe he'd served his sentence and left Cambodia. Perhaps he had bribed the police to let him out early. Either way, it looked like the man with the gold teeth was none other than Salama Massri, head archaeologist of this dig.

Clues were popping in and out of Jack's

head. He remembered finding a recording in Rachel Newington's house in Cambodia that suggested she knew the person who'd kidnapped her.

Maybe Salama and Rachel had worked in Egypt at the same time. Perhaps he was here looking for treasure, while Rachel and Max were guarding the diadem. The question was whether Massri also knew Max.

Then a thought struck Jack. Penny had told him that someone was hunting for his brother. What if that person was Massri? Massri was a greedy man who'd stop at nothing to get his hands on a priceless treasure. Maybe he knew that

Max had the diadem and was trying to track him down.

The only way to find out was to search for clues. Jack looked around to make sure no one was watching, then lifted the flap of a nearby tent and sneaked inside.

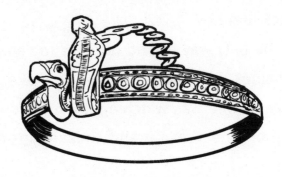

Chapter 9:
The Surprise Prisoner

There wasn't anything unusual inside the first tent, just some tools and empty crates. So Jack hurried along to the next one. In this one there were toilets and a mirror. Quickly moving to another tent, Jack found himself in some kind of storage area.

There were boxes of artifacts piled up at the side. In the middle of the tent stood a pole in the sand. Sitting against it with his back towards Jack was a young boy. His wrists were tied to the pole, and his body was slumped as if he were sleeping. Probably a worker who'd got in trouble for breaking something, Jack thought.

He walked round to check that the boy was OK. When he saw his face, he got the biggest surprise of his life. It wasn't just any boy. It was his brother, Max!

A rush of emotions came over Jack and he started to cry with joy. He couldn't believe that, after all these months, he'd finally found his brother. He hugged Max tightly, then sat back to examine him. Apart from the drool hanging down from his mouth, Max seemed OK. There weren't any visible wounds on his body.

Jack started shaking his brother by the shoulders, but Max didn't wake up.

He knelt down and put his ear to Max's mouth. Max was breathing, but he wasn't coming round. Jack wondered whether Massri had given him a sleeping potion. Reaching into his Book Bag, Jack pulled out his GPF Time Release Vapors – a tub of strong-smelling cream that could wake anyone from any kind of sleep. It was perfect if someone had been drugged, or had bumped their head and was unconscious.

'One whiff of this,' Jack said to his brother, 'and you'll be all right again.'

Just as Jack lifted the tub to Max's nose, there was a noise outside the tent. It was a girl, and she was coming closer.

'Get off of me, you lug!' she yelled.

Quickly Jack put away the Time Release Vapors and hid behind a stack of boxes.

The tent flap opened, and the girl was tossed face first onto the floor. Oddly, she was carrying what looked like a GPF Book Bag. Massri stepped inside, just behind her.

'I told you and your mother to leave me alone!' he shouted.

Jack's ears pricked up. That was an odd thing to say. He noticed at the girl's hair. It was brown and curly, just like—

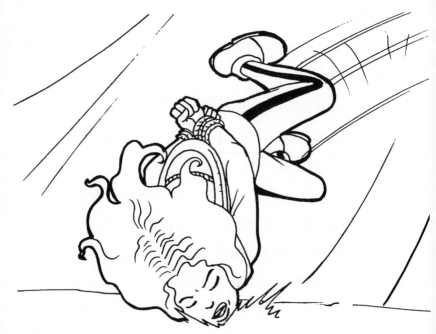

'Chai!' Massri called out.

His henchman entered, holding a rope. He yanked the girl off the floor and dragged her over to the same pole as Max, tying her wrists to it. It was then that Jack finally saw her face.

It was Kate – the girl he'd met in Cambodia! What was she doing here?

Before Jack could do anything, Massri and Chai were heading for the tent flap again.

'I'm closer than ever to finding the diadem,' Massri muttered. 'I know it's in Giza.'

'You'll never get it!' cried Kate, trying to break free.

'Oh yes I will,' he said. 'And when I do, I'll make sure I get rid of you both.'

Massri laughed an evil laugh. Then he and his thug left the tent.

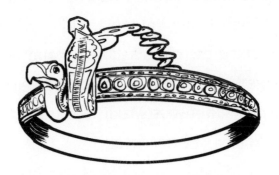

Chapter 10:
The Dynamic Trio

For a moment Jack sat there, stunned. This was a crazy coincidence. Max and Kate in the same room?

Jack moved towards Kate. When she saw who it was, she was excited and confused.

'Jack!' she said. 'What are you doing here?'

'Me?' he said. 'I'm here to save my brother. What are *you* doing here? And why are you wearing Max's Book Bag?' He pointed at the familiar backpack on her back.

'For your information,' said Kate, 'this is *my* Book Bag. I'm here for the same reason — to rescue Max.'

Jack wrinkled his brow in confusion.

'After meeting you I decided to join the GPF,' said Kate. 'You inspired me; plus, it was my only hope of seeing you again.'

Jack's cheeks grew hot. 'So finding my brother is your mission?' he asked.

If it was, Jack was going to have a bone to pick with Director Barter: he didn't understand why the GPF couldn't have asked him to take this on himself.

'I guess it was too risky to send you,' said Kate. 'You're family, after all. That could cloud your judgement.'

Jack's eyes narrowed. But before he could say anything, Kate carried on.

'Plus,' she said, 'I've got a bit of a reputation within the GPF. I'm one of their best secret agents.'

Jack highly doubted that. He'd never heard of Kate being an agent: he was the most decorated one. He'd stopped no less than thirteen criminals in a few short months.

'I've pretty much beaten your record,' said Kate. 'And I'm known for getting out of sticky situations.'

Jack looked at her bound wrists.

'Doesn't look like you're doing a very good job now,' he said.

'Give me a minute,' she said.

She closed her eyes and started to wriggle her shoulders. Like Houdini escaping from a straitjacket, within seconds Kate had maneuvred her wrists free. The ropes slipped down her arms and onto the floor.

Jack was impressed. He usually relied on the pocket knife from his boot to saw through rope.

'How did you—?' he began.

'It's a secret,' said Kate with a wink. 'Now let's get your brother out of here. After all, I didn't allow myself to be captured by that creep for nothing.'

Now Jack knew what Kate was doing in this tent. She had tricked Massri into capturing her so that she could get closer to Max.

Jack pulled out the Time Release Vapors and wafted them under his brother's nose.

Kate untied the ropes around Max's wrists. Within seconds he opened his eyes and saw his little brother.

'Jack!' he said, throwing his arms around him. 'I knew you'd come. You must have got my note.'

'Yeah, I did,' said Jack. 'Sorry it took me so long.'

'Better late than never,' said Max, smiling. 'How are Mom and Dad?'

'Great,' said Jack. 'They still think you're in Switzerland.'

'That was Director Barter's idea,' said Max. 'Pretty clever, huh?' Rubbing his wrists, he turned to Kate. 'Who are you?'

'I'm a friend of Jack's,' said Kate, winking at Jack, 'and a fellow GPF agent.'

Max looked at Jack, then at Kate, then back again. 'Friends, huh?' he said, raising an eyebrow.

Jack blushed for the second time. He changed the subject. 'Where's the diadem?' he asked.

'I buried it at Giza,' said Max, 'between the Sphinx and the Great Pyramid. I had to hide it from Massri. He's been trying to find it since it turned up in Thebes. You know,' he added, leaning closer to Jack and Kate, 'Salama is the son of Omar Massri, the guy who stole it from Howard Carter in the first place.'

Jack's eyes widened. That explained why Salama Massri was so desperate to find it.

'The problem is,' said Max, 'Massri knows where it is. He injected me with truth serum. I was forced to tell him its location. He may have already found it,' he added.

'I don't think so,' said Jack, remembering what Massri had told Kate. 'If we hurry, we might be able to beat him to it.'

He looked around the room. 'Where's your Book Bag?' he asked Max.

'I buried it near the diadem,' said Max. 'I didn't want Massri to get his hands on that either.'

'Clever,' said Jack.

Kate stood up. 'You boys spend way too much time chit-chatting,' she said. 'If we're going to stop Massri, we have to get going.'

Jack and Max looked at each other. Neither of them liked being told what to do by a girl. But Kate was right: they had to hurry. They dashed out of the tent and

found themselves in the middle of the
compound. Massri and Chai were
nowhere to be seen.

'Giza's more than three hundred miles
to the north,' said Max. 'Up river.'

'We can take the Longtail Boat,' said
Jack. After all, he'd just successfully
navigated it from Cairo.

He led Max and Kate towards the dock,
then dropped his toy boat into the water.
It ballooned in size once again. The trio
climbed in, and Jack started up the motor.
He cranked up the speed, heading up the

Nile as fast as he could.

Soon Jack's thoughts turned to Massri. Mr Hassan had said that whoever wore the diadem would have the power to 'rule the world'. Jack didn't know exactly what that meant, but he knew it meant trouble. They had to stop Massri from getting his hands on it – whatever the cost.

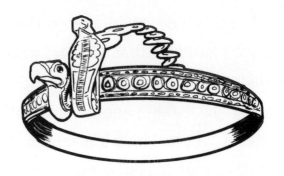

Chapter 11:
The Fateful Discovery

Jack, Kate and Max arrived at the dock in Giza. Jack put the Longtail Boat away. They turned and saw a sign:

SEE ONE OF THE SEVEN WONDERS
OF THE ANCIENT WORLD –
THE PYRAMID OF KHUFU

✳

BASK IN THE MAJESTY OF THE SPHINX

✳

ONLY 10 MILES SOUTHWEST TO GIZA

'That's where we're headed,' said Max.

Kate opened her Book Bag and pulled out her Flyboard. After she'd snapped it together, they all stepped on.

Kate programmed the Flyboard to 'NOTHING BUT AIR', and soon they were off. Travelling at twenty m.p.h., it didn't take them long to reach the Giza plateau.

Jack got off, and found himself staring at the most amazing monuments he'd ever seen.

Towering above him was the Sphinx, the largest statue in the world. It was taller than ten men and nearly as long as forty. Behind the Sphinx was the Pyramid of Khafre – the second largest of the pyramids at Giza.

'I buried the diadem in a small box,'
explained Max, 'near the Pyramid of
Khafre. We can find it with the
Transponder.'

He tapped on his Watch Phone, and
soon a map of the desert floor came up.
A tiny red dot started to blink on the
screen.

'This way,' he said, striding off.

Jack and Kate followed Max as he went past one of the paws of the Sphinx and headed towards the pyramids. Just then, Jack spied something in the distance. It was two men. One of them was digging in the sand.

'Wait,' he said, pulling Max back. 'That looks like Massri.'

Sure enough, it was Massri and his Asian assistant, Chai.

'I can't believe it,' said Max. 'How did he get here so soon? And how did he find the diadem without the Transponder?'

'I don't know,' said Jack, pulling his Tornado out of his bag. 'But we can nab him with this.'

The GPF Tornado was like a hand-held catapult. It could fling ropes out over a huge distance, ensnaring the bad guys. Jack set the dial to '2' and pulled the trigger.

ZIPPP!

Two ropes shot out. Unaware of the threat, Chai pulled a small box out of the ground. He handed it to his master, who opened it. Massri pulled the diadem out of the box, and put it on his head. A golden ring shone out around him and his assistant.

BLAM!

The ropes immediately bounced off the protective halo and then changed direction. They were now heading back towards Jack, Max and Kate!

'Run!' yelled Jack.

Massri laughed when he saw the three children scrambling for cover. 'You'll never take the diadem from me!' he shouted. 'It's my destiny to own it!'

His eyes grew cold, and he focused
them on Max. He spoke – and the words
sounded like they came from an ancient
language. A bolt of fire darted out of the
mouth of the cobra that decorated the
crown.

HISS!

It blasted Max in the thigh and sent
him spinning. Hurt and disoriented, he
fell to the ground.

'Max!' yelled Jack as he dived towards his brother. Max was still conscious, but barely. Quickly Jack turned to Kate. 'Get him out of here,' he said. 'Don't worry about me. I'll deal with Massri.'

Kate wanted to stay and help Jack, but she had no choice. Her mission was to save Max. She scooped the older boy onto the Flyboard and flew off.

Jack took his pocket knife out of his bag and waited. As the first rope reached him, he swung hard.

WHACK!

He cut it in two.

SLICE!

Jack struck yet another blow. The rope was now in four pieces. Luckily it was now too short to wrap itself around him. But the second rope was heading his way.

In the distance, Jack spied a solitary toilet block for tourists. If he could reach it, he might be able to shield himself behind the door. Jack made a break for it, but he wasn't fast enough. The second rope grabbed him by the foot and tripped him up. He fell to the ground.

In no time Jack was bound from head to toe. The rope left only two small holes over his eyes and mouth.

Massri came over, laughing.

'Technology is no match for ancient
power,' he said, then turned to his
henchman. 'Chai!' he ordered.

The next thing Jack knew, Chai was
dragging him off into the desert. Through
the small slit over his eyes, Jack could see
a bit of where he was going. Ahead stood
four makeshift tents.

Chai dragged Jack into one of the tents.

'Thanks to you,' said Massri from
behind Chai, 'I don't have to waste my
time tying you up.'

Then, laughing, the two men left.

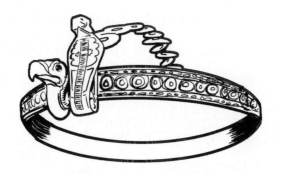

Chapter 12:
The Eavesdropper

Great, thought Jack. This was probably the first time in GPF history that a secret agent had been nabbed by his own gadget. The other agents were going to have a laugh about this one.

Jack tried to wriggle free but, as he'd expected, the rope was too tight. He tried to get his teeth around it, but there was no way he was going to be able to eat his way out. With any luck, Max would recover from that nasty shock, then he and Kate would come to find Jack.

In the meantime Jack had time to think – and listen. Over the course of the next hour, several people came in and out of the tent.

'How long until the President gets here?' said a man.

'He'll be here within the hour,' replied a woman.

'What about the secret service protecting him?' asked the man.

'They'll be no match for what Massri has planned,' said the woman, and then they both left the tent.

Jack wasn't sure what they were talking about. But whatever it was, it wasn't good news. The woman had mentioned 'the President'. Jack knew that there was a President in charge of Egypt.

Soon, other voices started whispering in the tent – children's voices.

'Jack,' said one. It sounded like Max.

Jack peeked out of the small gap in the rope. Sure enough, it was his brother. He breathed a sigh of relief. Max had recovered quickly. He and Kate must have tracked him using the Agent Tracker device embedded in their Watch Phones.

'We're going to cut you free,' said Kate.

Jack could feel rustling by his side, and soon the ropes around him relaxed. He shook his body, and they fell off.

'Are you OK?' said Jack to his brother.

'Yeah,' said Max. 'Kate took care of me and revived me with some Time Release Vapors. Sorry it took so long.'

Jack noticed the backpack on Max's back.

'We dug up your brother's Book Bag,' Kate explained. 'We thought that three lots of gadgets would be better than two.'

'There's a lot of commotion outside,' said Max. 'Any idea what's going on?'

'I heard some people talking,' said Jack. 'The President is coming.'

'What is Massri up to?' asked Max.

'Let's check it out,' said Jack.

The trio sneaked out of the tent. The desert was crawling with people. There were workers setting up a podium and rolling out a red carpet in front of the Sphinx. News crews were scrambling everywhere. Snack stands were open for business. Whatever Massri was planning, it looked like it was going to be big.

'Where's Massri?' asked Kate.

Jack opened his Book Bag and pulled out his Google Goggles. He placed them over his eyes, and switched the magnification to *ZOOM*. He scanned the

desert, but there was no sign of Massri or Chai. He then switched it to X-Ray. Massri wasn't in any of the trucks or tents.

'He's not here,' said Jack. 'But the President's coming. He'll be here within the hour.'

'Plenty of time for us to formulate a plan,' said Max.

Jack, Kate and Max discussed how they were going to capture Massri. By the end of the hour, they were ready.

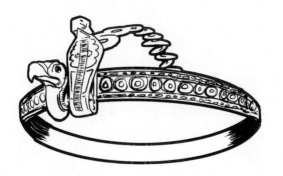

Chapter 13:
The Army

A voice rang out from the crowd. It was an Egyptian man in a suit. He was listening to instructions from an earpiece in his right ear.

'The President of Egypt is coming!' he said. 'Everybody take your seats!'

Hundreds of people raced towards the stands. A black stretch limo pulled up to the red carpet. The President of Egypt stepped out of the car, with Massri and Chai walking behind. The fact that the

President was standing so close to Massri complicated things.

'We can't nab Massri without hurting the President,' said Jack.

'Let's be patient,' said Max, 'and see what happens next.'

Massri and the President walked up to the podium. Massri leaned towards the microphone, and the crowd began to cheer.

'Ladies and gentleman,' he said. 'Today
is a historic day for Egypt. After years of
searching, I have finally found King Tut's
missing diadem!'

The crowd roared with delight.

'Stolen, more like it,' Kate whispered to
the boys.

The President of Egypt stood proudly
next to Massri. Chai handed Massri the
box with the diadem in it. When they saw

the box, the children gasped in dismay.

'We have to stop him before he puts it on!' said Max.

As Massri opened the box, Jack, Max and Kate dashed towards the podium. The man placed the diadem on his head and the golden halo appeared. He lifted his hands to the crowd.

'This is the power of the diadem,' he said. 'An impenetrable shield that protects whoever wears it!'

The President of Egypt looked confused.

'For years I have been searching for this diadem,' Massri explained, 'to avenge my father's reputation. And now it has come back to the Massri family. With this crown,' he added, 'I will rule the world!'

The President didn't like what he was hearing. He turned nervously to Massri. 'I think that we should call off this press conference,' he said. 'Perhaps we can discuss how you feel about your father with the help of a – a doctor . . .'

But Massri was having none of it. He ignored the President. 'Unleash the army!' he yelled.

The heavens parted, and an ancient voice boomed across the sky. Jack, Kate and Max stopped in their tracks in front of the podium. They looked to the east. The sand was starting to move. It was making a clicking sound.

'What's going on?' asked Jack.

A piercing scream came from the crowd.

'Scorpions!'

Sure enough, hundreds of huge scorpions were scurrying up out of the sand and coming their way, tails lifted, ready to strike.

The secret service men grabbed the President and threw him into his limo.

The journalists were part reporting, part scrambling for cover. Men and women were sprinting for their cars. Everyone was screaming.

'You can run,' yelled Massri, 'but you can't hide! My army will find every last one of you, and force you to bow to me, your new leader!'

Within moments the scorpions had swarmed all over the place. Their tails darted forward, trying to poison whoever they could. Several people fled for the

Pyramid of Khufu. Others hid behind the paws of the Sphinx. The President's limo tried to leave, but the scorpions had surrounded it, their tails tapping at the windows.

Jack, Max and Kate's plan to capture Massri had failed. They hadn't reckoned they'd be facing a scorpion army.

'How can we stop them?' yelled Jack over the screaming crowd.

'Let's squash them!' said Max, pointing to a large heap of boulders near the pyramid.

Jack turned and saw in the distance a thirty-feet-high pile of rocks left over from previous digs. They were tied together by sturdy rope netting. Jack knew that the only way to kill a scorpion was to step on it. The three agents sprinted for the rocks.

As they did so, a scorpion's tail darted

at Jack's ankle. He dodged aside before it had a chance to sting him, and looked over at Kate. A huge scorpion was closing in on her too.

'Watch out!' he yelled.

Kate reached into her Book Bag and pulled out her Flyboard. She whacked the scorpion with it.

BLAM!

It stepped back and shook its head, then focused its eyes angrily on Kate.

CRUNCH!

She smashed one of its pincers. 'Take that!' she said as she hopped onto the Flyboard and took off.

Jack and Max got on their Flyboards too, and the three of them zoomed towards the boulders. Unfortunately for them, Massri had spotted them.

HISS!

A blast of light shot out the diadem and hit the back of Jack's Flyboard. The engine caught fire, and it spun out of control. Jack flew off and tumbled to the ground. He groaned in pain, but quickly got his feet.

'Oh no you don't!' screamed Massri.

Max and Kate were now hovering at the base of the rocks.

HISS!

Massri sent a bolt of light towards Max. It missed, instead burning through one of the ropes holding the boulders. The rocks shifted and crunched together.

Massri was furious. He ordered the scorpions to attack the children. Hundreds of the creatures gathered together and swept towards them.

'I'll distract them!' yelled Jack to Kate and Max. 'Release the rocks when I say!'

Kate and Max nodded, then rose to the top of the boulders. The pulled their Laser Bursts out of their bags and waited. Jack grabbed a tissue out of his pocket and waved it to attract the scorpions' attention.

'Over here!' he shouted.

A wall of scorpions headed for Jack. Massri turned to his assistant, pleased with the turn of events.

'They'll never survive,' he said as he headed towards the limo. 'A perfect moment,' he added, 'to tell the President it's time to hand the country over to *me*.'

As soon as the scorpions were close enough, Jack called up to Kate and Max. 'Cut the ropes!' he cried.

Kate and Max shone their Laser Bursts, and easily sliced through the thick rope. The boulders began to rumble, then tumbled to the ground. Like a giant wave, they rolled over the scorpions, sending

them flying and crushing every last one. Jack dived out of the way and narrowly missed being flattened.

When Massri saw what had happened, his face grew purple with rage. 'How dare you!' he hissed, heading after Jack, blasts of light shooting from the top of the diadem.

ZAP!

Jack zigzagged through the sand.

BLAM!

A blast of light narrowly missed him, but Jack knew there was no way he could keep running for ever. Then he had an idea.

BLAM!

Another blast of light missed his foot by inches.

'Jack!' screamed Kate. 'Wait for us!' But Jack couldn't stop. There was no going back. He reached into his Book Bag and pulled out the Mini Bomb. He stopped and turned round to confront Massri.

'You'll never rule the world!' he yelled.

He threw the Mini Bomb in Massri's path. It exploded, creating a small crater. Massri tripped and fell to the ground. The diadem popped off his head and rolled about ten feet away.

This was exactly what Jack had been hoping for. He dashed towards it, but Massri got there first.

'This will be the end of you,' he sneered at Jack, lifting the crown towards his head again.

Just then, a loud screech came from above. Jack looked up. It was a bird of prey, just like the one he'd seen in London and at the Egyptian Museum. It was soaring high in the sky.

All of a sudden the bird dived with its talons outstretched. *Not again*, Jack thought to himself as he dropped to the ground. He put his hands over his head.

SWOOSH!

Jack felt the air whoosh past his ears, but nothing touched him. The falcon hadn't struck. He risked a peek. Massri was standing before him with a frightened

look on his face. He was no longer
holding the diadem.

'The King's falcon has spoken . . .' he
muttered.

SCREECH!

Jack looked up and saw the bird
clutching the diadem in its claws.

SCREECH!

The falcon flew down towards Jack and
dropped the diadem into his hands.

Jack was stunned. He looked up at the bird soaring peacefully above him once more. Maybe instead of trying to hurt Jack back at the museum, it had been trying to communicate with him, telling him to come to Egypt and save the diadem!

When Massri saw Jack holding the crown, he turned and ran. But a whirling rope thrown by Max was coming his way. Before Massri could escape, it had wrapped itself around him, and he fell to the ground with a thud.

Max and Kate were zooming towards him on their Flyboards. Max was carrying the Tornado in his hands.

'Nice work,' he said, slapping his brother's back.

'Thanks,' said Jack. 'I had a little help from a . . . a friend.'

The bird gave one last screech down to Jack, and then disappeared into the sky.

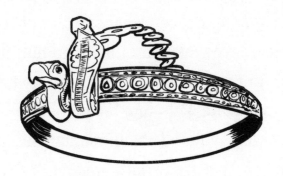

Chapter 14:
The Goodbye

The Egyptian police soon arrived, and dragged a cocooned Massri into the back of a police van. They threw his henchman, Chai, in behind him.

'Well,' Jack said to Massri, 'so much for ruling the world, huh?'

Massri mumbled something that sounded a lot like, 'You haven't seen the last of me.'

A policeman slammed the door in his face and climbed into the driver's seat.

With a rumble of the engine, the van quickly drove off, and with it, one of the most sinister villains Jack had ever faced.

'I guess we can return the diadem to Mr Hassan,' said Max. 'For a while I didn't know who to trust.'

'Why don't I do it?' offered Kate. 'After all, you boys need to get home.'

Jack smiled at her. 'Thanks,' he said.

Kate began to tap furiously on her Watch Phone. 'I hope you don't mind . . .'

she said. 'I told the Director I'd call.'

The screen on her Watch Phone sizzled. Jack peered over her shoulder as an image of a man appeared. It was the same man he'd met in Gerald Barter's office in the Arctic. Now Jack knew the true identity of his boss.

'Hi, Director,' Kate said, speaking into her wrist. 'The package is safe.'

'Good work, Secret Agent Starlight,' he replied.

Jack had never heard the code name 'Starlight' before. Suddenly Director Barter noticed Jack and Max in the background.

'Hello, Secret Agent Courage,' he said to Jack. 'I knew I couldn't keep you away from Egypt for long.'

Jack smiled at the Director, hoping he wasn't going to get into trouble for muscling in on Kate's mission.

'Happy to see you too, Secret Agent

Wisdom,' said the Director. He was talking to Max.

When Max had told Jack about his missions, he'd never mentioned his code name. For an older brother, 'Wisdom' was a perfect fit.

'Where's the diadem?' the Director asked.

'Starlight is taking it to Mr Hassan today,' said Max.

'Good work,' he said. 'All of you. Director Barter signing off.'

Then the screen went black.

'Well,' said Kate, holding up the diadem, 'I guess I'd better get this to Mr Hassan. It's been great,' she said to the boys.

'It's been good working with you too,' said Jack. 'I'm glad you became a GPF agent.'

Kate smiled, then threw her arms around him.

As she pulled back, she planted a kiss on his cheek. Jack blushed. Max cleared his throat.

'Maybe we can visit you in Cambodia,' said Jack. He really hoped he'd get a chance to see Kate again.

'I'd like that,' she said, smiling.

'Say hi to your mom for me,' said Max.

'I will,' she said as she waved goodbye and turned to leave. 'Wish me luck on my next adventure!'

The boys watched Kate until she was out of sight.

Jack turned to his brother. 'I've been waiting for months to say this,' he said. 'Let's go home!'

He took the Portable Map out of his Book Bag. He opened it out and put it on the ground. Pulling out a small flag of England, Jack stuck it on the right place. He grabbed his brother's hand and held on tight.

Jack yelled, 'Off to England!' A brilliant light flashed, and he and Max disappeared.

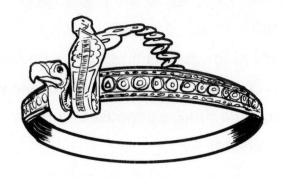

Chapter 15:
The Trip Home

When they returned home, they found
themselves in Jack's bedroom. There was
a knock at the door.

'How's the homework going?' came
their mother's voice.

Jack and Max looked at each other. Jack
started to giggle. If only his mom knew.

'Great,' he said. 'Come in and I can
show you.'

The door opened. When Corinne saw

Max standing there, she nearly fainted from the shock.

'Max!' she exclaimed as she ran over to him. She hugged him tight. 'What are you doing here? You're supposed to be in Switzerland!'

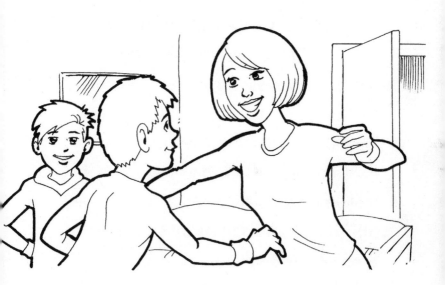

Max pulled a note out of the pocket of his jeans and handed it to his mother. 'This is for you,' he said. He winked at Jack.

Corinne's eyes scanned the note. 'It's a letter from your principal,' she said. 'It says your school had to close down because of money trouble. He's going to arrange for you to go to our local school. Well, why didn't he tell me this before?' she said crossly. 'Sending a young boy alone on a plane is dangerous!'

'It's OK, Mom,' said Max, trying to calm her down. 'An escort travelled with me.' He winked at Jack again. 'I was in good hands.'

Corinne sighed deeply. 'I suppose the most important thing is that you're safe.' She looked around Jack's bedroom, confused. 'Where are your bags?'

'In my room,' said Max.

Jack knew that Max was fibbing, but Max had said it so confidently, his mom had no choice but to believe him.

'And tomorrow is your twelfth birthday!'

Corinne cried. 'What terrific timing! Your father will be pleased!'

In all the commotion, Jack had forgotten about Max's birthday. His mother was right. Perfect timing indeed.

Corinne dashed out of the room. 'John!' she called as she bounded down the stairs. 'Guess who's home!'

Max turned to Jack. 'Thanks again,' he said. 'For everything.'

Jack smiled at his brother.

'I'm going to go and check out my room,' said Max. 'I hope Mom hasn't painted it pink.'

Max made his way to the door, and closed it behind him.

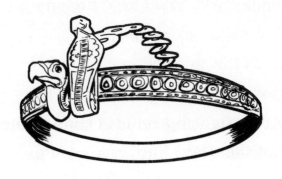

Chapter 16:
The Decision

Jack paused for a moment and let everything sink in. After all this time, his mission to find his brother had finally come to an end. And he was tired. Really, really tired. During the last few months Jack's body had been pushed to the limit. He'd nearly been gobbled up by a dinosaur, stung by deadly jellyfish, eaten by a polar bear and beheaded by a master illusionist.

Going over to his computer, Jack signed

on to the GPF secure site. He quickly typed the following email:

Dear Director Barter,

After fighting no less than twelve criminals (and a dinosaur), I've decided to leave the GPF. I want to be a normal kid. I want to hang out with my friends. I want to be able to read a book without having to go off on a mission nearly every night. If you need me, you know where you can find me.

Sincerely,

Secret Agent Courage

Jack moved the mouse to push the SEND button. But something stopped him.

What was he thinking? He didn't have to quit the GPF. After all, he loved being a secret agent. And since Max and Kate were GPF agents, they might be able to go on more missions together. Perhaps he could just take a break.

Jack added 'for a few months' after the part about deciding to leave the GPF, and pressed the SEND button.

Putting on his pajamas, Jack crawled under the covers and looked at the glow-in-the-dark stars on his ceiling – the ones his dad had bought for him and his brother, Max.

'Goodnight, Max!' he shouted happily.

A voice came from the room next door. 'Goodnight, Jack!' said Max.

Jack smiled. Thinking that was the best thing he'd heard in months, he closed his eyes and fell into a deep, satisfied sleep.

SECRET AGENT NOTES